The Little Snowflake

by Steve Metzger

illustrated by Monica Wellington

SCHOLASTIC INC.

New York   Toronto   London   Auckland   Sydney
Mexico City   New Delhi   Hong Kong   Buenos Aires

To a peaceful world
for all children
— S.M.

For my little dancing snowflake, Lydia
— M.W.

ISBN 0-439-55656-2

Text copyright © 2003 by Steve Metzger.
Illustrations copyright © 2003 by Monica Wellington.

12 11   7 8/0

Printed in the U.S.A.
First printing, December 2003

It was a cold winter's day. Up in the sky, the Little Snowflake was inside a big, gray cloud.

"When I reach the ground," he said, "I want to be a part of the biggest and best snowman in the world!"

The Little Snowflake looked down. "It's a long way to go . . . but I'm brave," said the Little Snowflake as he jumped.

Falling and tumbling through the sky, the Little Snowflake saw many other snowflakes whirling and twirling. Some had simple patterns and some had fancy designs, but all of them had six sides.
What a beautiful sight! he thought.

On the way down, the Little Snowflake bounced off another snowflake. "Move over, buddy!" the other snowflake shouted. "Watch where you're going!"

"I'm sorry," the Little Snowflake said. "I didn't mean to bump into you."

The Little Snowflake kept falling and falling. Suddenly, he landed on something with feathers.

This can't be the ground, the Little Snowflake thought. *It's too soft.* Looking down, he yelled, "It's a goose! What's going to happen to me now?"

The goose was flying with lots of other geese. They flew in the shape of a giant V. First the geese veered left, then right. Suddenly, they began to flap their wings to go very fast.

Oops! The Little Snowflake fell off the goose.

"Here I go again," he said.

Falling and falling, down, down, down.

"I hope I land in that big meadow over there," the Little Snowflake said.

"It will be the perfect spot for children to build a snowman . . . with me in it!"

Falling and falling, down, down, down, closer and closer to the ground.

"Here I come!" the Little Snowflake yelled.

Finally, the Little Snowflake *did* land in the big meadow but not on the ground.

"Oh, no!" the Little Snowflake said. "I've landed on a big stone. What will happen next?"

The Little Snowflake watched as some children began to gather nearby.

"Let's build a snowman," Anna said.

"That's a great idea," Jacob added.

"Yes!" said the Little Snowflake. "A *really* great idea!"

Anna made a snowball and began to roll it across the snow. The snowball grew bigger and bigger.

"This snowball's getting too big for me to push by myself," Anna said.

"I'll help you," Greg said.

"Good job, kids!" the Little Snowflake called out. "Don't forget about me."

But the children didn't hear or see the Little Snowflake.

The snowball grew so big that Julia and Jacob needed to help roll it. The children pushed the big snowball toward the Little Snowflake. "Oh, boy!" the Little Snowflake said. "Now they'll roll that big snowball over here and pick me up. Then my wish will come true."

But before they reached the Little Snowflake, Anna shouted, "Stop!"

"What's going on?" asked Jacob.

"Look, there's a stone," Anna replied. "Our snowball might break apart if we roll over it."

"Okay," Greg said. "We'll stop here. Now, let's make the middle part."

"I'm still here!" the Little Snowflake cried out. Then he sang this song:

Look at me! Look at me!
I'm down here on this stone.
Please put me in your snowman.
Don't leave me all alone.

But nobody heard the Little Snowflake's song.
The Little Snowflake sadly looked on as Julia, Jacob, and Greg rolled the
snowman's middle while Anna rolled the smaller snowball for the head.

After they stacked the snowballs, Greg said, "It really looks good!"

"No, it doesn't," the Little Snowflake said to himself. "It doesn't look good at all."

"But our snowman's not finished," Anna said. "It needs two eyes, a nose, and a mouth."

"And me!" the Little Snowflake shouted.

"Let's use these two rocks for eyes," Julia said.

"And these little rocks for the mouth," added Jacob.

"Here's a carrot stick for the nose," said Greg. "I had an extra one in my lunch bag."

"Now it's really done," Anna added.
All the children stood back to take a good look at their snowman.

"It still doesn't look right," Julia said. "It's missing something." She looked down and noticed the Little Snowflake on the big stone. "Look at this!"

"It's a snowflake," said Anna. "And he's all by himself."

The Little Snowflake began to smile. He couldn't believe the children were looking at him.

"Let's use him for our snowman," Greg said.

"But where?" Jacob asked.

"I know," Julia said, carefully picking up the Little Snowflake. As she placed him on one of the rocks, she said, "He'll be the twinkle in our snowman's eye."

The Little Snowflake smiled his biggest smile.

The children stood back to take another look at their snowman.
"Now it's the best snowman in the whole world!" Anna said.
The other children agreed . . . and so did the Little Snowflake.